The Ugly Duckling

❧ Fairy Tale Treasury ❧

Adapted by
Jane Jerrard

Illustrated by
Susan Spellman

Publications International, Ltd.

One fine day in May, a duck sitting on her nest felt something move underneath her. Her eggs were hatching! One by one, her ducklings broke through their eggshells, and each was yellower and fluffier than the one before.

Finally, the last egg cracked open. The duckling that came out was large and clumsy and a dirty gray color. He did not look like the other ducklings at all!

The mother duck thought, "How big and ugly he is! I wonder if he is a turkey chick." But she loved him just the same. And when she led her babies to the pond, the ugly duckling swam just as well as the rest, so she knew he could not be a turkey.

The next day, the proud mama duck took her babies home to the farmyard for the first time.

When the little family entered the farmyard where the fat ducks and geese lived, the other birds were quite rude.

"Look at that ugly little fellow!" said one white duck—and bit the duckling on his long neck.

The other birds teased the poor duckling. Soon, even his own brothers and sisters called him "ugly" and wouldn't play with him.

As the days passed, the duckling grew more ugly, and the teasing got worse and worse. Finally, he decided to run away.

The duckling wandered through fields until he came to a swamp where wild geese lived. Before the duckling could speak to the geese, some dogs came and they flew away. The ugly duckling hid in the weeds, for he was too frightened to leave.

As soon as he was sure the dogs were gone, the lonely little duckling set off again, looking for company. At last, he came to a little hut, where an old woman lived with her cat and her prize hen. She took the duckling in.

But the cat and the hen were mean to the duckling. Besides, he was a wild bird, and although the hut was warm and dry, he longed to be out on the water. So one fall day he ran away to find a lake.

And find one he did. He was happier on his lake, though the wild ducks there would not speak to him. One day, a flock of beautiful birds flew by. The sight of them made the ugly duckling cry, though he did not know why.

Soon afterward, the wild ducks flew off, but the duckling stayed. It grew so cold one night that the duckling awoke to find his feet frozen in a sheet of ice!

Luckily, a farmer found the duckling there and freed him from the ice. The kind man took him home, thinking the bird would make a fine pet for his children.

But when the farmer set the duckling down in his kitchen, the noisy children frightened the bird, and he ran and ran around the room. What a mess he made! The farmer's wife chased him right out the kitchen door.

The frightened duckling did not run far, for it was dark and cold outside. He found a hiding place and made a nest for himself. There he spent the whole winter, trying to keep warm and coming out only to search for food. It was the longest, loneliest winter you can imagine.

Finally spring came. The duckling stretched his neck and flew to his little lake.

Just as the lonely bird started to swim, three swans appeared from out of the shadows. As the duckling drew near, he bowed his head. But when he lowered his eyes, he saw the most beautiful swan of all. It was his own reflection!

The ugly duckling was really a swan! You see, it doesn't matter if you're born in a duck's nest, if you come from a swan's egg.